This book
belongs to

NAUGHTY NICE ?
☐   ☐

Written by Holly Lansley.
Illustrated by Lara Ede.

The Naughty List

Lara Ede (Nice) • Holly Lansley (Naughty)

make
believe
ideas

Dearest Mister Santa Claus,

We NEED to have a chaT.

That time I put
my sister's make-up
on our old cat
CLOVER,
my Sister Said
I'd RUINED her Stuff,
but the Cat LOVED
her makeover!

make-up

I also planned a NICE surprise, and painted Gran's house blue. You should have seen her walls before — they looked like old BEEF STEW!

The School wrote Mum a letter and she seemed a little sad, So I hatched a plan to show her that I'm really NOT that Bad!

Dear Mrs McCrumb,

We're writing to inform you that your son has been very naughty. On school picture day, he cut the hair of several students, but conveniently left his own intact. Parents of the students are very unhappy with ɪ

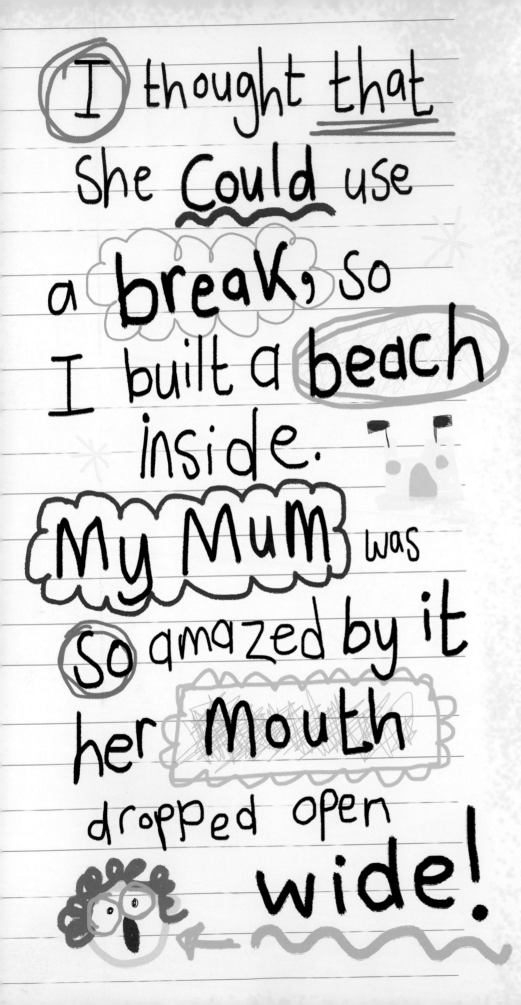

I thought that she could use a **break**, so I built a **beach** inside. **My Mum** was **so** amazed by it her **Mouth** dropped open **wide!**

So **now** You KNow How Good I've Been, Write down on Your SCRoLL:

Lastly, IF there's
Room LeFT,
there's One More Thing
I'd like!

Pretty Please

With Cream

on top...

...Can I have a Bike?!

Thanks and Merry Christmas.
Love from
Tom McCrumb
x
Shiny Red
Super speedy!